Original title: The Kind Panda

First edition: January 2020

www.childrensbookcrew.com

this
book to
belongs

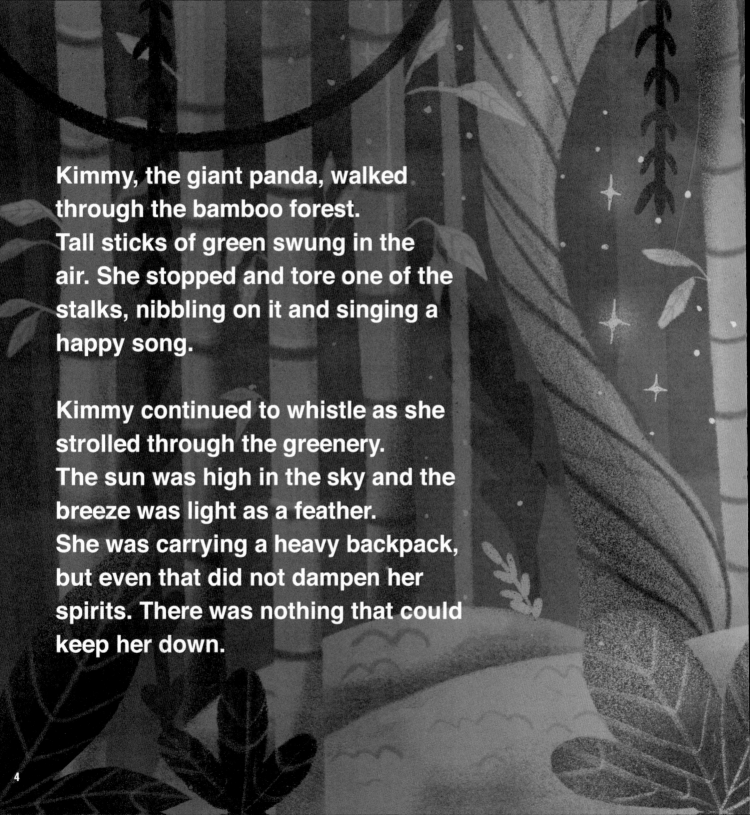

Kimmy, the giant panda, walked through the bamboo forest.
Tall sticks of green swung in the air. She stopped and tore one of the stalks, nibbling on it and singing a happy song.

Kimmy continued to whistle as she strolled through the greenery.
The sun was high in the sky and the breeze was light as a feather.
She was carrying a heavy backpack, but even that did not dampen her spirits. There was nothing that could keep her down.

Far off in the distance, there came a crying sound from one of the trees. Kimmy decided to investigate.

When she got to the tree,
she could see a red panda high up in the branches.

"What's wrong?"
asked Kimmy from the ground.

"I lost my money," the red panda said. "I had it, and then I looked, and it was gone. I was supposed to buy a new blanket for grandma panda."

Kimmy looked up into the eyes of the red panda and then dipped her hand into her bag.
"You can have my money," she said.

"But I'm only a stranger,"
said the red panda.

"You need it more than I do," Kimmy said. "I can see it in your eyes."

"I don't even know if I can pay you back," the red panda said.

"That's okay," said Kimmy.
"Pay me back if you can."

Kimmy wandered off,
singing another happy song...

IT IS FUNNY,
FUNNY, FUNNY.
I HAD MONEY, MONEY, MONEY.
BUT I HAVE NO NEED.
NO, I HAVE NO GREED.
SO I SPREAD IT AROUND
LIKE HONEY.

11

RAWRRRR

The sound came from behind
Kimmy. She spun around to see
who was there.

The sound was louder this time.
A snow leopard bared its teeth,
inches from Kimmy.
She had not even seen it coming.
She closed her eyes and hoped.

Kimmy opened her eyes again.
This was not a roar of anger – it was
a roar of pain. Kimmy looked closer.
The snow leopard had its tail trapped
under a rock.

"You poor thing," said Kimmy.
"I am not poor," said the snow leopard.
"I am fierce and dangerous."
"Let me help you," said Kimmy.
"But what if I eat you?" asked the snow leopard.
"You like to eat sheep and goats," Kimmy said.
"I'll take my chances.
You need help,
so I want to help you.
You can decide what
to do after that."

Kimmy walked around the creature as it growled at her. She grabbed hold of the rock and used all of her strength to remove it from the snow leopard's tail.

The snow leopard looked at Kimmy
for a moment before growling once
more and running off into the bushes.
Kimmy walked on, singing another
happy song.

LEOPARD, LEOPARD, LEOPARD,
HOW POOR YOUR TAIL.
I'M THE ONE TO HELP YOU
WHEN OTHERS WOULD
SURELY FAIL.
I LIFT THE ROCK.
AND STAND IN SHOCK.
YOU ARE MUCH FASTER
THAN A SNAIL

"That's a silly song,"
said a snub-nosed monkey.
It was sitting on the path
in front of Kimmy.

"Good afternoon to you, Mr. Monkey,"
said Kimmy.

"It is not a good afternoon,"
said the snub-nosed monkey.
"It is a miserable afternoon."

"The sun is shining," said Kimmy.
"The sun is too hot."
"The breeze is gentle," said Kimmy.
"The breeze is too tickly in my ears."
"The forest is so lush and green,"
said Kimmy.
"I hate the color green."

"Do you know what I think?" said Kimmy. "I think you must be hungry. I know I get a little cranky when I haven't had enough to eat."

"You don't know anything," said the monkey.

"Well, how about I leave this lovely stick of bamboo here, along with these three peaches I found earlier?" said Kimmy.

"What are you going to eat?"

"I will find more food," said Kimmy, and she walked on as the monkey pretended not to be interested.

Kimmy sighed. She was finally home. Her small house sat in the middle of a bamboo grove.

She had helped a lot of people today, but now she had arrived home with no money and no food, and it was late.

It was her birthday, but she had no one to share it with.

Kimmy's mood dropped. She thought she must be the only animal left in the forest who liked to help people.

Then she heard the sweetest song in the world. A happy birthday song rang out, and three animals poked their heads out from behind the house.

"We made you a cake,"
they all said together.

"I bought the ingredients,"
said the red panda.

"I added the peaches,"
said the snub-nosed monkey.

"And I baked the cake,"
said the snow leopard.

"We found each other in the forest.
You had helped each of us and asked
nothing in return.
We wanted to try helping too. So we
made you a cake for your birthday.
We ask for nothing in return."